Creative Sparks

"Spectacle the hidden Talents

Flairs and Glairs

Publication House

"Creative Sparks"

"Spectacle the hidden Talents"

ISBN No: 978-93-90799-14-5"
1st Edition
Language – English and Hindi

Flairs and Glairs
Publication House
Regd. Under MSME Act.

Disclaimer

This is a work of fiction and solely represent the thoughts of the corresponding authors of the articles. Our editors have tried their best to edit the content of all the authors and check the plagiarism.
All the write-ups in this book are unique and are only published in this book.
In case any plagiarism or error is found, only the author is responsible alone, and not the publisher or the Compilers.

Cover Designing and Book Formatting
Shubham Shah and

Acknowledgement

We heartily thank the almighty for giving us the strength, wisdom and grace to unbolt our ideas & thoughts into mesmerizing words. This would not have been possible without the blessing of our beloved Parents. We sincerely thank this universe for shooting down the best family who trust us in all our decisions and encourage in chasing the dreams. They are the pillars on which we're standing at the peak. As per this book, we would like to thank the publishing & editing team for their guidance and continuous support, this wouldn't have been possible without Shubham Shah Sir's constant support who is the founder of Flairs and Glairs Publication and our extended thanks to Shobhit Kumar Sir who is the manangement head of the same for helping us whole heartedly. And also, we would like to thank Ishani Agarwal Ma'am who is the co-founder of the publication for guiding us in this project. We would likewise love to include all the Co-authors who have carried away their cherished time to join our journey and made wings to our aspirations. We are short of words to show our passion and gratitude towards all as working towards a goal was a united effort that will always be and none of them left any stone unturned to compose the best out of their inks and imaginations.Thank you to each one of our readers for appreciating our work. We deeply indebted for the love and support you all show us.

Co-Authors

Shubham Shah (Founder Flairs and Glairs)
Ishani Agarwal (Co-Founder Flairs and Glairs)

1. Antaripa Talukdar (Compiler)
2. Manash Pratim Bhatta (Compiler)
3. Abhimanyu Arya
4. Abhishek Dutta Chowdhury
5. Ananya Srivastava
6. Ankit Rath
7. Ankita Singhania
8. Aruna Shukla
9. Ayesha Ayub
10. Bhuvaneswari Anandan
11. Bijoyata Nandi
12. Charvee Vyas
13. Dr.Arshi Khan
14. Dr.G.Akshay Vivek
15. Gayathri T
16. Gourav Kumar Sharma
17. Haripriya Tiwari
18. Karishma Bisht
19. Khushi Parekh
20. Killamsetty Sravanth
21. Layashree A. Venkatesh
22. Maherin Nasir
23. Manash Jyoti Choudhury
24. Mirza Akram Baig
25. Mohini Awasthi
26. Numana Khan
27. Parineeta Das
28. Partha Pratim Borkataki

29. Payal Surani
30. Prachi Khanna
31. Pranav M Sreejith
32. Rutupurna Satapathy
33. S.D. Rahel Chiru
34. Saumya Mishra
35. Sayani Bag
36. Shriyangana Pyne
37. Siddhi Channe
38. Sneha Raj
39. Snehal Apturkar
40. Swagatika Sahoo
41. Tusar Ranjan Mahapatra
42. Udit Jain Kothari

Shubham Shah

(Founder- Flairs and Glairs)

Shubham Shah, an entrepreneur at “Flairs & Glairs” a brand with dynamics in events organizing and cultural educational pan INDIA, is a 26yrs old guy who recently has entered the digital platform of imprinting emotions. He has initiated with his own open mic platform to help budding poets and aspiring writers under his brand named as “Teekhe Zasbaaat”

He is a commerce graduate from the Bhagalpur City of Bihar.
He states Writing has impersonated him since childhood and he has now been writing for over a decade!
Cooking, on the other hand, is his passion! He also mentions, trying out new things just tickles him!
When asked sir, Why SPICY EMOTIONS?
He smiled and added, "agar jasbaat teekhe na ho toh wo jasbaat kahan" Spices are all that blends! So do his words!
As a chef, he presents to you his dish! Hot and freshly served! Taste it! Feel it! Enjoy it! You can also find his writing in the Book "Teekhe Zasbaaat" and 50+ Co-authored anthologies. With his passion to explore opportunities across Platforms, he is working with keen devotion and We wish him all the very best for his future ventures.
He is Featured in the **International Magazine De-Mode** for his upcoming solo novel.
He is **Approved by Ne8x for its Lit Fest,** and is a **Golden Star Awards 2020 Winner.**
He is an **India Book of Records Holder** for his Anthology **Satrang,** and has the **Grandmaster** title by **Asia Book of Records**, for the same.
He has also been featured in **Prabhat Khabar**, **Dainik Jagran** and other renowned Newspaper for his achievements.
He has also been awarded with **India Star Republic Award 2021.**
He has been a proud co-author to
India Book of Records (Title- Black)
World Book of Records (Title -15 Wonders of Poetries)
India Book of Records (Title - Aaina)
Vajra World Records Holder (Title - Gustakhi Maaf Hai)
High Range of Records Holder (Title - Gustakhi Maaf Hai)

Share your reviews on his

INSTAGRAM

@spicy_emotions
@shubham4shah

Or via email on

shubham2shah@gmail.com

To stay tuned to his work and opportunities follow his business Handles

INSTAGRAM FACEBOOK YOUTUBE

@flairsandglairs
@teekhezasbaaat

WEBSITE:

https://flairsandglairs.in/
https://flairsandglairs.com/

Ishani Agarwal

(Co-Founder- Flairs and Glairs)

Ishani Agarwal hails from the City of Joy, Kolkata.
She is the co-founder of her Community "Teekhe Zasbaaat" and Flairs and Glairs Publication.
Been a Compiler for 45+ Anthologies, she is in the process for more. Co-authored in 150+ Anthologies. She is a India Book of Records Holder, a Vajra World Records Holder, a High Range of Records Holder and a Bravo Record holder.

Approved by Ne8x for its Lit Fest 2020, and Literary Icon 2020. Also a Golden Star Awards Winner 2020.
She has also been awarded with India Star Republic Award 2021.
She has been featured by the National Magazine "Taree Zameen Par" with the title 'unstoppable'.
Also featured in the International Magazine DeMode for her upcoming solo novel, she is proud to write on social issues, and is happy with the love she is receiving.
Connect with her on Instagram: @Ishani_agarwal_quotes / @compilations_so_far

ANTARIPA TALUKDAR (COMPILER)

Myself Antaripa, Born and raised in Guwahati, Assam; The City of Temples. A vorocious reader and an amateur writer. Currently pursuing my Post Graduation in Commerce. Being always passionate about Art & fascinated by creative quirks with firm believe that everything that happen has something worth experiencing to me. I love to play with words and write from the depth of my heart & express my emotions by framing new words; keeping them simple for readers. My writing has been published previously in many anthologies and I also enthusiastically participate in many writing activities and inspire young for creative line "Write every penning's with a Spark because Writing is a way to say one's feeling out" "Creative Sparks is my First Anthology as a COMPILER"

Follow me @antaripa_talukdar,
www.yourquote.in/antaripatalukdar OR
Write to me at antaripatalukdar44@gmail.com

Creative Sparks

There is more to Creativity
Than rhythm and rhymes
It is a door to our soul,
Which is undiminished by flow.
It's a place where sorrow and joy
Are deeply expressed.
It is the thoughts which can be ordinarily confessed.
Sometimes we like to think
To capture the ideas in Ink.
The pen begins to flow,
And leave our thoughts to glow.
It's when the mind starts to fly free
We really do begin to see the sky beyond the tree.
Creativity can make almost anything
Become immortal
But despite of being mortal,
By poetic words we're becoming immortal.
We see the place where ideas grow.
The One's passion we must show.
As creative ideas take us to the top
Don't keep them locked up in
Dark non-stop.
Put down the thoughts to Spark
Because, when we have inspiration
We'll be adding our part out of darks
To the whole of creation
Making Creative Sparks.

Side By Side I Found My Pride (The Best Version Of Mine)

Being the best version of yourself is quite feasible and it is one of thing that almost all people wish for.
We people want to go through life knowing that we have a tendency to but aren't passing by opportunities.
We want to Know that we are giving our best efforts and getting the most out of every moment.
"Truly happy and productive individuals get that method by changing into the most effective, most real version of themselves they will be. Not on the outside but on the within. It is not a Joke or something but It's concerning reality. This may Sounds straightforward, I know.
It's an easy construct.
The matter is, it's totally arduous to try to do, it takes plenty of desireness, and it will take a lot of willingness to work it out. Nothing to do in life is ever simple. If you would like to try to do nice work, it's attending to take plenty of diligence to try to do it.
And you are going to possess to interrupt out of your temperature and take some possibilities that may scare the crap out of you.
"My goal to find the " best version of mine" is not that easy.
It seems like i adopted a threadbare phrase straight from a self-reformation book as my motivation in life.
However, I attribute the development of this desire.
And, In order to become the best version of mine, I Has to do something that 99% of other people will not do because of Fear, laziness, etc.
First, I need to find me balance
that means i have to be happy about myself.
Secondly, I had to embrace my weaknesses and laziness.
Though, not all weaknesses are continuously dangerous however, some can be used as strengths.

Laziness on the other hand can be improved upon slowly by gaining control on itself. However, to be the "best version of mine"

I had to learn,(learning can be new or it can be a further learning)to improve myself. Learning something new can be a scary experience but experience is damn vital thing to seek out oneself within the "best version".

So, I noticed my "best version" in Writing.

The secret to writing is actually quite simple; All you need to do is to express enough about your thoughts like an open diary who carves emotions well when it comes to writing.

Writing is actually a way to say your feeling out.

The "best version of mine" I found in writing so, i write to express myself. As i love writing some of the writing which i wrote are of my life phase.

I was making an attempt to figure out my life and at last i found that in writing wherever I specify my emotions through words.

The passion for poetry had made me spectacle the world through an altogether different prism which symbolizes my personality.

"Hence I found the best version of mine"

MANASH PRATIM BHATTA (CO-COMPILER)

My full name is Manash Pratim Bhatta. I belong to the Guwahati city of Assam. I'm a Commerce graduate. This is my first Anthology Project as a Co-Compiler. My writings has been published in few other anthologies also. Writing is one of my greatest passions which I follow whole heartedly and always believe that the path of writing leads to explorations of different diversities in life. I always try to distribute the fragrance of positivity among everyone in the society through my writings and I'll be really very happy and glad if I become successful in this mission. Please visit my Blog Website 'www.explorewithmpb.blogspot.com' where you all can find my creative contents associated with Poetry, Travelling and few other topics.

Email ID : bhatta.manash2.0@gmail.com
Instagram Username : manashbhatta

With The Passion Of Cooperation

With the passion of cooperation we support each other,
In exploring the universal realities that can open our eyes with truth;
With the passion of cooperation we realise each other's needs and requirements,
To share our wisdom and wealth with each other,
With the passion of cooperation we help each other in discovering the ideas,
That can stop the destructions and replace them with creations;
With the passion of cooperation we assist each other in designing the roadmaps,
That can direct us towards the purpose of our lives;
With the passion of cooperation we can guide each other in improving and developing,
The health and psychological powers of everyone,
To build up each other enthusiastic, intelligent and joyful citizens;
With the passion of cooperation we can even afford to establish,
A magnificent empire of humanity in our society;
Let's keep this passion alive forever,
And join each other's hands to solve the problems of our surroundings,
Together with a team spirit and integrity,
And journey towards the destination of peace, harmony and success;
With the aim to make the world a better place to live in.

The Art Of Creative Writing

Creative writing can be considered as an art as well as a science. It is a kind of skill that everyone possess inside. But it's the duty and responsibility of a person to search and find out this talent inside his/her own brain. It is a kind of hidden aptitude. I'm stating all these from my own experience in my life. Anyone can write anything with his/her creative imagination. It can be a poem, a prose, a quote, a short story, a micro-tale or anything. But at first, the person have to imagine something regarding a concept using his/her own brain. It requires tough patience. It takes time to write a content with one's own creation. It requires hardcore concentration and determination of the person in that particular topic in which he/she is trying to write something. And most importantly he/she should possess immense interest and passion in writing as well as in that specific topic. People can only concentrate in those subject matters in which they have interests. To build a strong interest in writing, a person must read creative writings of other writers on newspapers, magazines and anthologies. He/she can also create interest in writing by reading a variety of books of different authors. He/She can also read different blog articles in internet. Moreover, one can even read a lot of beautiful creative posts of a lot of people nowadays in social media as well for building his/her interest in the field of writing. These points really inspires a person to write a lot of new things on various themes and genres in his/her day to day life by using the magic of creativity.

Creative writing defines the mentality of a particular writer. The writing style of a writer determines his/her thought process. The kind of language and specific words he/she uses identifies the viewpoints of the writer regarding the particular concepts and subject matters he/she mentions in his/her writings. It can even point out his/her likes and dislikes. It

can depict about the philosophies and ideologies the writer follows. Thus, it can be stated that creative writing can always help a person in expressing his/her feelings, emotions and point of views about any topic by providing him/her the opportunities to pen down his/her thoughts through written words and present them in front of the readers vividly.

ABHIMANYU ARYA

His name means heroic. He's a law student from Manipal University Jaipur. He's an avid reader, photographer, writer, traveller and a polyglot. He's fond of typewriters as well as fountain pens and is always up for an adventure.

Email ID : abarya99@gmail.com
Instagram Username : @abhimanyuarya99

Unpredictable Life

We're here today but tomorrow where will we go?
We don't even have any clue, Life ahead is unpredictable which is absolutely true.
I continue to deal with several thoughts in my mind,
Even my directionless heart doesn't know what to find.
I'm probably like a flame ignited battling with the strongest breeze,
Or like a wanderer moving somewhere with certain ease.
With the hope of finding my way out of this chaotic maze,
Where life can be welcoming with the arrival of a new phase.

Reverence

Surrounded by all the trials and tribulations, I stand before you to take my burden away,
My reverence for you is so strong that no poweful force can snatch it away.
All the unrelenting thoughts continue to bother me like nothing else,
There's only hope to follow the right path, that's what my heart has to say.

ABHISHEK DUTTA CHOWDHURY

Abhishek Dutta Chowdhury, from Allahabad, is currently pursuing, Master's in English Literature from University of Allahabad. He is a shy 'Ink Soldier' who contends a constant struggle with his 'Self' within the silent chambers of his spirited psyche. His words are fueled with underived intrinsic emotions that explain the psychological perspectives of simple everyday occurrences and events.

Email ID : abhishekduttachowdhury71@gmail.com
Instagram Username: abhishekduttachowdhury1608

The Protagonist of the Pandemic-Tale

She is a sailor, sailing across the Perplexities of the post modern inhibited water course,
Umteen lengths long.
Running parallel to continuous chain of events,
Past, present and future.
The blank verse of the epidemic virus,
Challenges her potential-potency by greatly increasing,
The responsibilities of,
The Abode and the World outside.
The dusty corridors of reality,
Mirrors the realm of chaos.
Where she doesn't have the choice,
The freedom to leave the battle field like the Staminate-male,
And hide within,
The four walls of the sensitive soul-cabin,
For a numerical-moment to rest her spirited state of existence.
Because,
She is a Mother.
The Protagonist of the Pandemic-Tale.
A complex Superhero,
Known worldwide for taking,
The strangest decisions of life.
Using her,
Conscious Cardiovascular,
Instant Heart-beats.

A Twist in the Tale

He was at the PVR cinemas, waiting for, the movie to start, enjoying the advertisements when His Bae
texted him.
She: Hey Baby you know what happened today!
He immediately stood up.
She: So today I hurt My leg,
Lost My nail polish.
I broke My nail.
It was bleeding.
I had a stomach ache.
They didn't have My favorite pink color dress, Can You imagine that!
You know how much I love My skin right?
Right?
Hey why aren't You replying?
Must be with your Ex.
Ohh that Bitch!
I saw My Facebook notification today.
You checked into PVR.
Ohh! Now You are ignoring Me ha!
She must be holding Your hand Isn't that so?
Oh you must be kissing her!
Why did You cheat on Me!
Why?
Fine I also have some self respect.
I am going back to Ranveer.
Atleast He was so loyal to me, unlike You.
Go suck in Her Hell Embrace till Doomsday!
I am breaking up with You.
And She blocked Him
After 52 secs .
"Jaya he, jaya he, jaya he,
Jaya jayajaya, jaya he!",

He said and sat down to have a look at his Apple Phone's LCD screen, and started sobbing.
"Hey Hey, kid calm down.There I see, you are so strong. I understand, I also get very emotional every time I hear the national anthem. A series of goosebumps, runs through my body.You are a proud Indian.
God bless you", someone patted on His shoulder.

ANANYA SRIVASTAVA

Ananya belongs to Amritsar, Punjab, INDIA. She is trying to express and understand the life norms through words. And she sits with the moon and stars to loose her mind, and find her soul.

Email ID : ananyasri311@gmail.com
Instagram Username : _the_unstoppable_pen

The Rain Does This To Us

You are no different than me
under the same sky, the same shadows.
You live a thousand miles away
somewhere in the suburbs.
Even though i am surrounded by the cemmented walls,
I feel the same.
And where the first raindrop pecks us
on the dry cheeks,
and grey clouds hover over our bent heads,
we're are one.
Pathetic beings, dying for a distraction as mystical as this.

The Outside World

The idea of the real, outside
world begins to form, where a week is left to
leave the school.
You'll begin to observe that it is nothing like,
the pink-painted walls of your tiny room.
it's vast and scary
the world you see peeping through your windows
will not care if you have a heart of gold.
The place for your feeling and secrets is your room,
it's walls
which helped you grow and
know each one of your tales.

ANKIT RATH

Ankit Rath is born on 7th Jan 2002. He believes the world can be a better place to live by spreading love and affection towards others.

Email ID : suvam7jan@gmail.com

Revolution of Technology

Mobile phones have really taken over our lives, isn't it. Well we don't like to admit that. Technology has made our life so easier than before. From waking up in the morning to going to bed we have our phones in our hand. A wise man once said, "Technology can be a very good servant but not a good master". Wherever you go be it public places, gyms, restaurants, malls people are sticked to their phones.The world of technology is full of 'aspirational things' means things which you don't have but want to have. No doubt why our insecurities are at peak these days because we always see such things around us. People out there on social media pretend to be perfect and by watching them you think your life isn't good as everybody else is. But that's not true because that's only a small fake aspect of what you see. Yes that's fake because those people be it celebrity, cricketer, fashion blogger they show you things which they want to, they show the positive and good part. That's what people do and everyone wants to be like that, because that's what people give a damn for, doesn't that sounds silly that we are running behind those contents. Well that's how technology has changed scenario of the society. Truth is that society doesn't give a flying fuck about you, it will sell you and show you every stupid thing. Be precise what you intake.

ANKITA SINGHANIA

Her name is Ankita Singhania. She belongs to the city of joy, Kolkata. Accounts manager by Profession with that she is pursuing Masters in Business Administration. Few months ago, she started to realise that" Pen and paper are their best friends." She started to express her thoughts in writings. Through her short quotes and poems she likes to motivate people to deal with their problems. She has a page in instagram where she writes her quotes.

Do follow Pen_paper19_07

Email ID : singhaniaankita27@gmail.com

Broken But Beautiful

Life is sometimes complicated, sometimes it is smooth ....
Life is sometimes worse, sometimes it is best....
Life is sometimes villain, sometimes it is Hero...
Life is sometimes Parents, sometimes it is Friends...
Life is sometimes Broken, but it will become beautiful ....

(2)

Sometimes, we just need a routine, a certainity, a logic to put our lives back together.... Thats it!

ARUNA SHUKLA

Aruna Shukla is Research Scholar of English literature at National Institute of Technology, Raipur. She has completed her masters in English Literature from Pandit Ravishankar Shukla University Raipur, Chhattisgarh. She is an inquisitive soul and loves writing her thoughts. She is rapacious reader and a dedicated teacher. She has a page on Instagram where she shares her thought.

Email ID : arunashukla95@gmail.com
Instagram Username : Weirdo0208

Perception of Beauty

I was born in a middle class family and had so many dreams since childhood. But as I grew up I had noticed one thing in a society which always bothered me and still disturbs me alot. It is the perception of beautiful women in society. Women with extra weight, under weight and dark colour are not accepted as beautiful women rather overtly criticised for the way they look and because of this they didnt feel secure and confident about their own skin. They are constantly forced to look in a certain way set by society. The thing which disturbs me a lot is that why can't they flaunt their beauty freely. Some of them have curvy hips, thick thighs and some of them have the sexiest waist and the beautiful skin colour but then also they aren't getting enough love from the society and their near ones. Women having all these qualities are still struggling to accept themselves because of the constant criticism they are facing. They are already having emotional ups and downs, kindly don't make it worse by commenting on their body type and skin colour. It's my humble request to everyone reading this if you can't make a person feel good about themselves then don't be a critique as well. Accept yourself because you are beautiful. Be generous, be kind, our World needs that.

Writing comes more easily if you have something to say,

Similarly you can't feel the sun without its rays
Life is full of ups and down
And you just have to adjust your crown.

AYESHA AYUB

Ayesha Ayub is an aspiring poetess, content writer and a medical student studying in Asian Medical Institute. Her hobbies include reading, writing and music.

Email ID : ayeshaayub4@gmail.com.
Instagram Username : ayeshasartsy

Brave, Never Bitter

You once promised me eternity.
Not a fleeting memory,
Gone with the wind.
Not a house of broken dreams.
A moment
One moment
Flickering flares of sadness,
Keep igniting wildfire.
Tired, torn, bleak and broken,
I collapse on vividity.
Parched on the highland,
I look upon the mainland.
Responsibilities burden my shoulders.
A fearless sword in hand,
I battle the clenched fists of hopelessness,
Into the night, I go
Wandering the meandering leaves of remembrance.
An instant
A flash
Scarred, blood stained with a bluish smile,
A wilted flower sits on the table,
Forever abandoned.
It sings the songs of loneliness.
Upon construing my existence,
Invites me for a cup of sanity.
A heart-to-heart conversation, maybe.
"Do you feel lonely?"
The flower blurts in silence,
"Do you feel pain as well?"
"Are you scared of the dark, too?"
Agaze, amazed
My eyes search for answers.
I feel your pain.

I know you're hurt.
I smile, apologetically,
"O Sweet Flower of the Morn,
Souls leave when the Sun dries out.
Conflict and chaos strip innocence.
Naked and soulless,
Sins the world on end."
"I feel lonely.
I feel pain.
The dark obliterates my being."
"Yet, I move forward.
I wake up.
I live.
I breathe.
I fight.
I make it right."
"O Sweet Flower of the Morn,
Your time will come."
"Loneliness is a mere excuse, we're always alone.
Pain is a fleeting memory that stings.
The dark is just the absence of light.
Brave hearts win battles,
In this war called life."

Love

Beaming lights of joy
Rose petals shower your gentle skin
Sun-kissed lilies bloom in your garden
Your smile becomes my precious thing
Eyes squint when darkness arrives
My heart rests when we're side-by-side

BHUVANESWARI ANANDAN

She is Bhuvaneswari Anandan. But People know her as Bhuvana Anandan from her blog and podcast called "Poetry Diaries". She is currently studying B.Voc.Digital Journalism in Loyola College, Chennai. She has worked as a content writer for a company and for a freelancer. Moreover, she loves to read books. Therefore, she has also reviewed a few books. Her hobbies would include reading books, painting, singing and writing stories, poems and songs in English. She also loves to travel a lot and my dream is to travel the world someday.

Email ID : bhuvanaau@gmail.com
Instagram Usernames : @uvanaa ; @poetry.diaries_

Believe Limitless

"Don't be silly there is no world beyond this glass house" said the insects mockingly to the butterfly. "Trust me, the world is limitless" she tried convincing them. But they never believed in her until one day like a miracle the door was open, she noticed and flew so high breaking the limits of the sky and all other insects watched her with their mouth wide open all while.

The Disguise

On a rainy night just before the dawn he kissed me under the sky and said "You are absolutely an angel". I smiled at him, took my knife slowly and slaughtered him. Then I looked down at his body and said "Be careful what you wish for, sometimes even the devil is disguised as an angel".

BIJOYATA NANDI

Bijoyata Nandi:20 , hailing from Guwahati, Assam. She's a student and currently she pursuing Biotechnology. Her hobbies is to create few words into a sentence and few sentences into a poem, basically she turns her hustle into words. Also she is a classical dancer/a Rabindra Nitika and she is beauty blogger in YouTube . She's someone who believes in "WE ARE NOT DEFINED BY WHAT HAPPENS TO US, BUT BY THE CHOICES WE MAKE".

Email ID : nandi.bijoyata@gmail.com

Untold Mysteries

It isn't so hard to find
But the way is invincible and blind
The path of the mystery lies
Infront of every eye.
Yet Homosapiens are not fortunate enough to find it in their own right.
One who has been collecting all proofs and signs
Wave mysteriously vanished from the earth's natural design.
Feeling easy is not an option.
Arising the lives worst recollection.
Memories that should have faded away years ago.
But still jaunts the time where the fate go.
Not far from the day, when it will be rediscovered.
Apart from God but a demigod will rccover.

On Being A Teenager

With the end of childhood
Here begins the life of spring.
With a hope for Life to be more exciting,
New hopes and new dreams
New desires and new wish,
Makes life more beautiful
With beautiful moments to cherish.
But with the harsh realities,
Life gets bitter,
Like the tunes.
From the torn strings of a guitar,
Beautiful were those wings.
That wanted to fly,
Wings of fancy and fun.
But misfortunate took every desire away.
A lot wind, a last soul
Sucking peace and positivity.
I'm it's own lost world.
Begins an arduous journey

CHARVEE VYAS

A writer who fades in poetic world feels splendid the love she has for poetry.

Email ID : vyascharv@gmail.com.
InstagramUsername : 2004notes

Mom & Dad

My love is not a lie ,
You are music of moonlight,
Lyrics of sunlight,
I'll make you flawless,
& I'll make you mine forever,
The rhythm of my heart,
Oxygen of my blood,
A magnificent shaayari,
A poetry to clench ,
You are the gleam of my life,
The love is hidden in infinity,
You hold me since day one of my life,
I am thankful to God,
Who has given me constants,
A great philosophers of my life,
You are architect of me,
I'll hold you in my heart,
Remember I repeat,
I'll hold you in my heart,
Love you beyond infinity,
Just to see you smile,
Till the day I die.

Nature

The morn,
The pleasant view,
Of sunrise,
When nature's beauty,
Is beyond everything,
In the evening,
Going upstairs,
Towards Terrace,
Just to feel,
The cool breeze,
To enjoy nature,
In solitude ,
In the night,
A blissful feeling,
When you forget,
The world,
Just staring,
The moon and stars,
And just feeling,
Remains,
Will be happiness.

DR. ARSHI KHAN

Arshi Khan is a Doctorate in English literature, lecturer at Integral University, Lucknow. An ardent reader and creative writer. Her poems talk of human nature, thoughts, freedom and liberation from shackles.

Email ID : khan.arshi19@gmail.com

We're Humans

We're humans!
We come, we go
We leave behind others to follow
We know not what's above
We know not what's beneath
We have the present, the present is we.
We cry and yell and laugh with glee
And hold the world's hand, in the possibly could be.
The heritage and vintage cars we love
We waste our lives going crowded clubs
We run to own and live to eat
We crime and thieve and boast and flee.
Our curdling hearts, have secrets and guilt
The ceaseless track fuels our kilt
We kill to survive, we gain to deprive
We shut the lil flicker
With two drinks upright!
We have Kindred Spirits and the Seven Deadly Sins
We embrace 'emall, we've no time to think
We gloat and glide and smoke and thrive
And the time going by, near the corner of life.
We judge and sin, we curse and win
We wait in despair to unclog affairs
The clock strikes eleven, we've not lived five
We're powerless and old and haggard to hide
The journey we take reaches the imminent
The passage though taken, makes it worthwhile
We fly, we swing, we cry, we grudge
It lies in our hearts to live or to nudge
We're humans! We just come once
We rise or we fall
'We' issue our chance worth living
If at all.

Little Angels

The early morning rise I see
With wind and cold and breeze and trees
Now as I set my armchair beside
and wish to see the impeccable sight
a one, a two, a three not more
come one by one, from three not four.
My little housemates I miss you so
The childhood filled your two and fro
The little movement of twigs and grains
The littering and fluttering of your lil reigns.
You filled me with such enormous joy
Your presence felt, however coy!
In tens and twelves you came and flew
My house alive with mist and dew
Now days have passed, I'm waiting though
For calm and quick your presence to show.
You were the right companion to be
The day's crowd now is not for free
The little neck movement, the glitter filled eyes
You picking in your trap, tiny food alive
Then as I steal to have you see
You flutter your wings and woosh!! You flee
Again that sight I wish I get
I wait with grains and drinks all set
The house attic aloof and wack
My tiny friends do come back.

DR. G. AKSHAY VIVEK

A Dreamy Physician.
Email ID:akahayviveklogandoctor1395@gmail.com
Instagram Username : vivek_akshay

Love Unchained

Neither Can You Promise Me Sunshine On The Horizon At Dawn!!
Nor Can I Promise You The Lush Of Crops To Be Born!!
But This Affection And Care In Between Is "Their Own" Unique Bond!!
"This Is LOVE My Darling!!",
Which Can't Get Carried Away Or Be Cheated Upon!!

Reality

In An Attempt To Stand Apart From Crowd,
We Tend To Get Lost Into Some World Of Bizzare Expectations!!
A Glimpse Of Our Reflection On A Broken Piece Of Glass Cries Out Loud,
"Abducted Are You From Thy Self To Fulfill Your Greedy Little Elation"!!

GAYATHRI T

Miss Gayathri.T began her writings with works of fiction in Wattpad. She slowly shifted her focus to expressing her feelings through poems and writings. Reading and writing from her school days, she is happy to connect to a lot of people through her writings. As an aspiring doctor from Karnataka, she has found quarantine useful to pen down her thoughts. She currently focuses on trying to voice the thoughts of the young minds.

You can contact her @g3doc123@gmail.com

Lost In Time

Waiting for you at our spot,
Dressed up a little, excited.
Smiling, awaiting your arrival!
You forgot about our routine
Lost track with friends.
Me, anxious as it gets late,
Checking my phone for a text or call.
Sighing, hurt a little, I sit on the ground
Looking at other couples together,
Enjoying time, so in love.
Giving excuses, I calm my heart
Easing the pain and hurt.
I go home shattered,
Were we loosing spark with time?
Late night, your reminder pops
"Anniversary date with babe" it read.
Sleepy eyes spring open
Lost, thinking, trying to reach me.
Me asleep in bed, phone silent
Tired after all the crying.
Somewhere in time, lost
Was the connection we once had.

Mask

They called us friends, well I was one to her...
But never the day would come,
when I would see the devil in her.
She played good, an excellent actress I must say,
Tried everything in power, to make me stay!
Well let's just say I wasn't dumb,
to fall head first into her trap.
I saw past her mask, and everything else became a past!
Never cried, never shed a tear,
For the loss of a friend so dear!
I saw her soul, and let her be,
Still my friend, that's all she gets from me!
She laughed and cried with me, in glee and pain,
Tried to clutch my life, but ended in vain.
I caught her twice, trying to stab my back
Everybody came to know, yet they turned their backs
Everything was perfect as though in a dream,
All fakeness filled my life during her realm.
She still lives today not knowing
That I know her secrets, like water flowing!

GOURAV KUMAR SHARMA

Gourav Kumar Sharma completed his schooling from SHHS in the town of India Railways hub and IIT, Kharagpur. He completed his M.Tech in Computer Science & Engineering at ITER Bhubaneswar. Landed up as an Asst. Project Manager to an IT firm within a short span with his hardship. Being an ICSE product apart from working he is extremely ingenious in every hobby he enrols. This makes him the master in whatever does. Understanding people & their cultures, Serving Humanity, Being Presentable, Raising Voice for women empowerment is part of his life. He says,"People at some point in life give up. All they need is a motivational voice & a little bit of care during the downfall." Gourav writes being their voice to make them rise again. The lockdown helped him unleashing the power of words & its connectivity towards serving humanity.

Email ID : gksharmaofficials@gmail.com.
Instagram : @gourav_kumar_sharma

Wonted Jones

In pain, you take in Acetaminophen,
In pang I induce spiffing write-ups.
For peace, you need to have Alcohol,
For quietude I write being matchless.
In low respiration you high Benzodiazepines,
I get my each breath via writing in a hush.
You have cymbalta as an antidepressant,
My words are stiff, habile enough to blow it off.
You have clozapine to lower risk of suicidal will,
Even when I am at top notch agony, I just write.
Hitherto! If you're still in unbearable torment,
Start writing, I pledge! it'll stop you to fall from grace.

Thy Flamboyance

Being Plucky on face,
Staying ballsy by gestures.
Foolhardy goes the citizenry,
By a wink of your angelic eyes.
The unflinching vocabulary you hold,
Makes the interviewer out of his flow.
You Swashbuckle everywhere you go,
Leaving the essence like an english rose.
Beauty with brain defines your presence,
Holding the fame & exemplar all around.

HARIPRIYA TIWARI

Haripriya Tiwari is an architect by profession but she is very passionate literature lover. She enjoys reading and writing. Her stress buster is to write and cook food. She enjoys to share her food with everyone but her poems with only close ones. Since from her childhood she always wanted to be a doctor but eventually she ended up with architecture and today she wants to be a part of architecture journalism where she can practise her knowledge and follow her passion towards literature. She started her journey of writing when she was of 11 years old to express her feelings herself and to hide it from world as she was introvert and a bookish insect. Today she is bold, confident and extrovert who loves to talk with everyone like chatter box and also likes to travel and explore the world.

Email ID : world.of.renu145@gmail.com.
Instagram Username : Priya.tiwari@145

My Treasure Is My Family

I'm feeling so happy and I don't know why?
I wanna laugh and even wanna cry.
I wanna tell something that I never said,
I love you mum and I love dad.
I'm missing you all, wanna you all tight
love you Di, Sonu and Bhai and i truly miss our silly fights.
I wish i can go back to my past and rewind all my life,
pause them and enjoy all those cute, funny, mischievous
phases our childhood life.
I wanna live those moments again,
from where that silly and foolish childhood began.
I'm so lucky that i have you all,
thanks for being with me at every rise and fall.
you all taught me what's wrong and what's right,
you have always taught me how to make my future bright.
without you people I'm nothing and might had lost,
whatever I'm today is you were with me at any cost.
I wanna thank you all from the bottom my heart,
thank you for everything and never let me be apart.

<u>"FRIENDS" Most Beautiful Treasure</u>

World's most beautiful treasure,
is term which always provides pleasure
They are our good luck charm,
and we know that they can never cause us harm.
They reach out our sorrows and they absorbs it,
they reach out our pain and dissolves it.
They helps us to create our dreams
where even monsters can't scream.
They are our stress relievers,
as also smile creators.
They never try to be the one,
who they think they can never become.
I like them because they are original,
they are shiny as a pearl.
They are our supporting sticks,
sometimes they do play funny tricks.
Being with whom is very enjoyable,
hope our friendship will always be stable
Please be with me in all my ways
you will be treasured for all my days.

KARISHMA BISHT

Her name is Karishma Bisht, she is working as an Assistant Professor in Isabella Thoburn College, Lucknow. She loves to research on new perspectives and is fond of applying creative pursuits in designing and content making.

Email ID : sunitabishtkari@gmail.com.
Instagram : masterthatenglish_17

Hush! Sush! Rush !

Hush! please stop, let me stitch this piece of cloth
I dwindled every thought in the shadow of my spot
Made indoor my prism to escape cataclysms
Prayed each day to fade my inscape of haze
Flashed light on the stone that spoke like my tomorrow…
Sush! please listen, let me wash it to escape
They Rushed in exiled frenzy in their primitive pace
Prayed each day to escape his wrath
Ostracised the one to frustrate on the other
Who cares if it's a minor or a mother
The master chants Hatty catty coolly to freeze you on the spot…
Rush! please listen, join me to see this stage
They lack divine vision but imitating his apparition
Prayed each day to kill with ammunition
Let's chant
"Charged a new light brigade"
"Charged a new light brigade"
Lobes turned mightier than loaded guns
Hush! Sush! can be history if our lobes rush has begun…

Goggledygook!

The time I thought the air was wild
The time amid your care.
Such hiccups felt like Goggledygook!
I know the starting pace is high
Then slower with the end of chase.
But Kindled in your act this far
This pace just felt like Goggledygook!
I know our blocks are building wide
With few more strands to bridge each day.
But in your eyes I see the calm
These waves just felt like Goggledygook!
I see the scales in the grip of time
My acts do quiver with change in state.
But such vibrations with your stick beside Makes all our pain seem Goggledygook!

KHUSHI PAREKH

Hi everyone, she is Khushi. She has opted for PCB as a career ahead & has played many sport games at various levels. she likes to write about deep & expressive things felt by her. except for writing, she is good at many other creative things which are of her interest.

Email ID : blackbelt.kp2017@icloud.com.
Instagram Username : @khushiparekh_16

Fry ends.

Feeling pleased as punch,
meeting my new friends,
it's totally different,
cracking jokes and surprising them.
I do feel like,
they all could be my close ones one day,
sharing tears and laughters,
anywhere and everyday.
Really annoying,when i think, what if they're judgemental,
or would envy me?
but for a gentle reminder,
I always wish them to be with me.
Listening to their life stories,
I would think mine is really tiny,
but isn't it fun,
exchanging secrets with unknown friends having different puns?
Running between the fields,
to enjoying unplanned trips.
I'll be with you,
but in tough times, please come and get through.
Will I be also left with happy pictures,
that will make me sad?
I feel like, it's only me
also afraid somewhere to see the real she.
After all this too,
I'll be glad,
thinking about the memories,
that we might have made.
It all seems so funky,
when everyone turns me into a crybaby.
but let's not go there and try to be fair.
I really wish to peep inside their minds,

and see what other people have described me to them,
what if they don't find the real me & I don't get redefined?
Even if I'm damaged totally,
I promise to not hurt anyone out there,
neither I intend to nor I'll pretend to,
or else I'd have no clue and rather prefer to be with you.

KILLAMSETTY SRAVANTH

Killamsetty Sravanth is a student studying in National institute of science and technology and currently taking up a bachelor's degree in computer science and engineering. He is interested in reading books which makes him to be more dedicated. He keeps on enjoying music mostly. He believes that life gives us multiple ways but to choose the right way is in our hands.

Email ID : killamsettysravanth962002@gmail.com.
Instagram Username : sravanth_killamsetty.

Quote 1>

Everything starts with ONE ~is you. And ends with a line ONE OF US

~the others who inspired from you. Start your journey!!!

Quote 2>

Planning will keep you perfect. Action will make you rise. Planning with Action take you to reach your destination.

Quote 3>

Every morning is a fresh morning for you because you don't know when your day is going to be fulfilled.

Quote 4>

When we get support, we feel better to stand wherever. If not we feel, no more scenes are left for us to rise up anywhere. All we need is a SUPPORT.

Quote 5>

HEAL YOURSELF FIRST AND THEN THE WORLD WILL HEAL FOR YOU.

LAYASHREE A. VENKATESH

She is a sixteen year old from Chintamani, Karnataka. She aspires to become a good playwright. She loves to dance, orate and write. She dreams of becoming a director and a playwright.

Email ID : layavenkatesh202@gmail.com
Instagram Usernames : @layavenkatesh ; @words_tangled

Part Of Us, Someday

She was a carefree, high spirited soul,
the entire society hated her for that.
She sometimes tried to be one of them, but none accepted her.
She once became a victim of an acid attack, it was her ill-fate or whatsoever.
She now completely was like them,
she moulded herself into the shape society desired,
but still society didn't accept her.
She's still trying to be one of them.
I hope she becomes one, someday.

Accept Her

Accept the way she is,
for you who have created it.
Accept her scar as beautiful,
as you have done it.
Every girl tries to mould herself
just the way society wants it.
But still it doesn't accept her
as how she is.
Why does the damn society has to
isolate a girl who has big scar on her face?
Why does it not try to understand
that she needs support, sympathy?
Many girls who are the victims of acid
attacks have scars and kept away.
Why? Doesn't society understand
what is she going through?
Please don't isolate anyone with any scar,
Cause you don't know what story she has behind it.

MAHERIN NASIR

She is 17 year old, trying to make something good out of her overthinking by penning it down. She's from Ranchi Jharkhand, just gave her boards this year (2020) even though she is a poet but she's still learning poetry. She hopes to get better and inshallah one day, people are gonna know her name.

Email ID : maherinnasir03@gmail.com.
Instagram Username : Inkedwithemotions

Deserted

I wish I could tell how it feels like to be alone around people. Like when I'm at school, all ganged up, everybody's talking about things going on in their lives but then I realise, I've really got nothing to tell them about although I've got plenty of things running on my mind. Or, or it hits when I'm waiting for my friends and they're late and every stranger that's passing by is giving me a look as if I don't belong there. Or, or it hits when I'm asleep and every night I dream or must I say, have nightmares about things related to death. It feels so sad how the things I used to love the most, couldn't make me feel about them in the same way anymore. It sometimes feel like this place, this world, nothing belongs to me. But I am still here, doing what is expected from me to do. Somehow I'm trying to just fit in, in the world where nothing makes sense to me, in a world where's place for me but I just fail to find it. I don't know if I'll ever be able to figure it out but I'll try. I'll keep trying in the hope that somehow someday something would make sense and I'll know it in just that exact moment, that this is what I've been searching for, that this is where I really do belong.

With You, I Found My Happiness

Just a year before,
Things were so different.
If you would ask anybody who knew me back then, they would tell you as if it feels like they don't even know me anymore.
Things happened with me that made me change,
Made me loose all my hopes,
Hopes to live, hopes to be happy again.
I had no dreams or ambition to follow or any desires to pass another day.
Until,
Until you came and filled this empty space.
You made me want to live and laugh again.
What can I even tell about you;
You're like another sun's ray
That gives me new hopes all the other day.
You held my hand when i was confused.
Between wanting to explore or ending my whole life.
You told me what's right,
Showed me my path and
Brought me back to life.
When I found you,
I found my happiness back.
Most importantly, found back my spark and met myself again.
Your cute little smile is like a cure to my heartache,
Even your crazy lame jokes could make me laugh till my stomach ache.
You're one of the best things
That has ever happened to me.
You didn't take a lot of time
And became like a world to me.
And in my world,

There's just you and me.
And today, I make a promise to you,
That I won't let anybody else ever come in between.
I can't explain what I feel for you,
I don't even want to.
Coz words don't matter,
Actions do.
And I promise that I'll never let you down,
And I will always love you true.

MANASH JYOTI CHOUDHURY

Manash Jyoti Choudhury belongs to Guwahati city, which is also known as city of temples from the state of Assam world famous for it's tea and the one-horned rhino. He is a Graduate in Commerce. He wants to convey his thoughts through his writing so that everywhere in the society fragrance of positivity spreads. Currently he is in search of good platform that would provide him opportunities to present his writing at a greater scale.

Email ID :manashjyotichoudhury1995@gmail.com

Fitness

Fitness in today's 21'st century has become a global issue. Today the life of the human being has become very hectic and complex. We are all running after money. We have crossed our stress limit due to which majority of the people are having depression and other health problems. Unnecessary competition has taken away our peace of mind resulting in poor relationship. Therefore it is essential to stay fit because when a person stays fit he will achieve his success. He will have a good relationship with others, a strong health and positivity. Now the question arise how to stay fit. The answer is very simple. First of all we have to take out time for ourselves and we have to divide our time into physical fitness and mental fitness. Physical fitness can be achieved by joining gym, yoga classes, running, jogging and other physical activities. We also have to change our food habits. We have to switch to healthy food from junk food and we have to avoid alcohol, smoking and tobacco products. And mental fitness can be achieved by keeping ourselves away from unnecessary emotions, thoughts and feelings. We have to think positive and act positive. We should not say "I can't do" instead we should say "I can do". Our motto should be"We Can We Will." A person physically and mentally fit can achieve success in life as physical and mental fitness are the backbone of human life.

MIRZA AKRAM BAIG

Mirza Akram Baig is a content writer, speaker and a co-author for many anthologies, including an anthology which is now "World Record Certified". His genre is mainly fiction, fantasy as inspired from J.K Rowling and Harry Potter series.

Email ID : akram12m@gmail.com.
Instagram Username : akram_mirza

Life Lessons From Harry Potter

Harry Potter has been my first and the most important series because of the great story and beautiful characters. Here's what some of the Important characters taught me

Albus Dumbledore taught me,

Greatness is achieved with great work and efforts. Good people work hard but great people work extra hard from the very start to achieve greatness!.

Lord Voldemort taught me,

Be careful while you wish for certain things in life, they maybe the reason for your downfall in the future.

Severus Snape taught me,

We often dislike people as they can be a bit controlling in life but it's for our own good and a hero can be anyone in disguise!.

RubeusHagrid taught me,

Looks can be deceiving. The real beauty of a person lies inside, like he treated his friends and creatures with love and respect.

The **Malfoy** family taught me,

Money and too much pride can lead you to misery, so always try to be modest in life!.

Hermione Granger taught me,

Studies are a very important part of our life and we can deal with any problem with good education!.

Ronald Weasley taught me,

A good friend is he who always has his friend's back in any situation and can do anything for him!.

Harry Potter taught me,

There can be horrors in your past. But it's your choices in life that are important, whom you choose to be with and the path you're headed with them matters!.

J.K Rowling taught me,

Magic do exist if you believe and one of her quotes taught me that

"Anything is possible if you have
a nerve" and I strongly believe in it!.

Dedicating these Lines to the Harry Potter Series that shows its Importace in My Life

Talk about "The boy who lived" and I will be brisk!.
Taught me in our world as well magic do exist!.
Made my childhood magical and made me more optimist,
Gave me a golden rule in life,
"What's life without a bit of risk!."

MOHINI AWASTHI

The name of the author is Mohini Awasthi. She is pursuing her Masters in English currently. She's ready for a wild adventure, accepting all the ebbs and highs of it. She is exploring numerous fields and testing the waters. She is in the process of writing her first fiction novel.

Email ID : mohini2598@gmail.com.
Instagram Username : @musings.with.mohini

The Tunnel

There was a city, enveloped with the hustle and bustle of a modern town with its shining lights, speeding cars, relentlessly occupied people, galloping streets, towering buildings and all the essences that paint a city. There were, however, some facets very peculiar to the place. Every neighbourhood had a complex, up and running machinery that looked like a gigantic tunnel. Whenever the grim machine whispered an unfortunate name, the body bearing that name was pulled by a force unknown, clutched, dragged and removed, until he/she stands at the mouth of the tunnel. Some people were summoned to this enormous reptile several times and the others, only once or twice, to decide their fate. Man, woman, or child, sane or insane, every being had been a guest to this befouled tunnel. The utter unnaturalness of it had made the endless loop, pretty natural. It was a starless night when Naman and his companions started to discuss the political preferences of each other. "I am not actually in support of all the actions of this government. Though, I do not completely deny the works..." began Naman. As soon as the words were out of his mouth, there came a horrific bombast of a cacophonous sound from the evil tunnel, announcing Naman's name. That was it. It was as if the tunnel sucked his body towards it. He tried to cling onto anything and everything but was forced to a stop only at the sinister entrance. Trying to catch his breath, he was dragged in. A huge crowd of people buzzed outside to watch Naman's misery. There was just a feeling of chaotic curiosity and inevitable eventuality among them, nobody pitied the boy. After an hour of screaming and screeching, Naman came out from the other end of the tunnel, 'anti-national' branded on his head, blood dripping down his nose, from the forehead. Everybody was horrified at the sight. The people at the back were standing on their toes to witness the

disaster. Then they scrunched their nose in disgust, some clicked their tongues, and some shook their heads in disrespect of the boy, signs of a label or two, or more, branded on each head. This tunnel had a big responsibility to label every person that went against the stringent norms and dictates of the society. The question, however, remains, who invented this machine? What bricks were used in its concrete construction? Actually, the tunnel was alive, flesh , blood and bone, made with the distinct features of all the people of the respective neighbourhood.

NUMANA KHAN

Her name is Numana khan and she has completed her intermediate studies from SKD Academy. She is pursuing B.A. from English Literature from ISABELLA THOBURN COLLEGE and its her second year. For her, writing her thoughts gives her both satisfaction and peace of mind. She has been writing since class IX.

Email ID : numzz20sep@gmail.com.
Instagram Username : numana_khan

WRITERS

Writers never let their wounds heal
Because pain teaches good lessons in real
From suffering their inspiration came
Then they mingle with their thoughts to find a sum
They forge themselves in fire
To get the best out of what they desire
They live in their own world of fantasy
Where everything comes up to them in a form of poetry
Hard to understand like persons they are
May seem unrated but their soul shines line an evening star
Sometimes people may say pathetic words to them
But the world knows they are the Earth's gem.

Imaginations

I wonder how in my mind i make up things
I wonder how i fly in the sky with my broken wings
There I went to the depths of my thought
Then I myself scratch all the past wounds i got
My pain comes out in a form of scream
And tears roll down like a stream
Flowing with, it takes me to a different universe
Where everything comes to me in a form of a verse
Then I sit under the sky thinking being still like a deaf and blind
Penning down whatever is whispered in my ears by the wind
Adding whatever says the pain of my wound
I love the universe all my wounds and imaginations have brought me in
Here I also apologize for my every sin
The love I got ,the hatred I went through
Everything is there on me like dew
Years passed, days are gone but everything happened to me is still fresh
But I stand brave like a proud flesh
Towards the end I concluded
In every situation and its survival my imaginations and almighty were only included.

PARINEETA DAS

She is Parineeta Das from Guwahati, Assam. Currently, she is pursuing B.com in Accountancy (Hons). She started her writing from her school days in the annual magazine. She loves to write because it's the way to express the untold words. She is not a professional writer but she loves her passion for writing. She lives mostly in her fictional world and writes mostly about those things. Other than writing, her hobbies are photography, singing and dancing too. She is also a good chef.

Email ID : parineetadas1999@gmail.com.
Instagram Username : parineeta12

Cartoons

Make me believe in imaginary world,
Doraemon's gadget, who make Nobita's life easy going
But no DORAEMON is in my life.
NINJA HATTORI's trick, which always help Kenichi
But no Ninja technique helps me.
Still, I believe to have DORAEMON and NINJA HATTORI with me one day.
Believe in TOM and JERRY's friendship, who never fails to support and fought for each other.
SHINCHAN's silly activities and his cute face, who makes everyone laugh and believe in life and enjoy
every moment which is present and not to worry about future.
But my silly activities always creates troubles and no one laughs also.
I am the duplicate version of half NOBITA and SHINCHAN.
FAIRLY TALES which make me believe in magical world and prince charming.
Still, I believe.

Ink of Pen

Allow my words to express,
brings the word library under a roof.
Reside happiness of every writer,
Sprinkle live to the words,
Silence of a person, turn into words,
Ink of pen..

Cherry Blossoms

It's not just a place,
it's not just a tree,
not just a color pink or
The blossoming flowers
Its dream of many people,
Home to many little ones
Place of peace,
where many families sit together and laugh
It's a place of love,
It's a place of happiness,
It's not just a tree, not just a place.

PARTHA PRATIM BORKATAKI

His Full name is Partha Pratim Borkataki. He belongs to Guwahati (Assam). He is a Commerce graduate, and he is also pursuing Company secretary course. He is a fitness freak and a foodie too. He is also running a Youtube Channel named Parth Borkataki Fitness where he tries to talk about fitness tips, show work-out videos and discuss about some motivational and philosophical concepts. Email ID : parthaborkataki.vv@gmail.com

Succeeding Along with Confidence

According to me, confidence is that element in our life which uplift a human being to the greatest heights of achievements or may even degrade a person to downfall. The most effective rule for confidence is honesty. It can be considered as the best tool to succeed along with confidence. It is because there is always two ways through which people tends to succeed. One is the path of honesty, truth, peace, passion and cooperation. The other one is the path of dishonesty, corruption, lies, greed and harmfulness. Now just imagine the results of both the ways adding the flavour of confidence in each one of them. It can be easily evaluated the first one will lead towards success and contentment in life. It's because honesty and confidence is really an awesome combination for achieving ultimate victory. Whoever chooses this path along with confidence will always cooperate with everyone and contribute a lot towards the betterment of the society confidently with passion without causing a single harm to anyone in his/her journey towards success. But a person who tries to move on through the second path with confidence will one day destroy himself/herself due to his/her own deeds. It will happen because people who chooses this path always tries to achieve success through dishonesty means, corruption and by harming others for their own profits. They don't have any positive feeling towards others' emotions and sentiments. These kind of people are simply hungry of money, fame and position. They don't have any kind of passion in their task. And as a result the society will also views them with the eyes of disrespect and hate. In this way only these type of people degrades their own morale in front of everyone. One can't achieve success without having a positive attitude, respect and cooperative mentality towards other people whom he/she deals with. Simply having confidence for all the wrong

reasons will never work. It will only make him/her guilty in future and can never provide him/her ultimate satisfaction in life. The next point is all about research and knowledge. Real confidence is mainly based upon proper research and knowledge in a particular field. If a person builds up self-confidence through these sources, he/she will undoubtedly win in his mission. It's because he/she can perform any task or solve any problem related to that particular field very easily and efficiently with confidence as he/she achieved complete knowledge and achieved expertism through proper research and hard work. He/she will become unstoppable in the race of perfection. But if a fellow shows confidence without proper research and knowledge in his/her field, it will be termed as over-confidence which is simply an illusion for him/her. In this kind of situation, he/she will face horrific failures in his/her way of life because having a little knowledge is not at all worth of building a man or woman perfect. This type of mentality of a person can't even help him/her in gaining one percent of success instead it will bring him/her lots of insults. Thus, I believe in this philosophy that having confidence is really great but having overconfidence is terrible. That's why confidence should always possess the ingredients of honesty, truth, passion, cooperative attitude, proper research and knowledge.

PAYAL SURANI

She is Payal Surani living in Vishakhapatnam. She had completed a diploma in computer sciences. Recently, she realized that she can pen down her thoughts too. So she just started engraving her emotions on a paper and instantly fell in love with writing. She can write poetries and short stories in Hindi and English as well.

Email ID : payal.surani99@gmail.com.
Instagram Username : payal.surani

Confessions of a wrecked heart

"Are you really going to leave without telling me what you've been dying to confess?" Her voice made him stop his running steps.

"Do you think I am that dumb to not recognise your selfless care or unconditional love for me in those pretty eyes. All that never-ending gazes of yours, the jealousy which was always reflected, the words you never spoke and the feelings you never articulated. They were so evident." She let out all at once and he stood there stunned by her words.

"Why don't you just accept the fact. Why do you keep on running away from me, even when you know you love me for eternity?" She paused for a while with tears filling in her eyes.

"You said you'd always be there for me. So when I needed you the most, where were you? Why weren't you there with me last night? I thought.." He did not let her finish this time.

"I was there. I was always there beside you. Just a bit far so you couldn't see me. I didn't want you to know about how I feel. I was terrified of my own feelings that started breathing inside of me. I never deserved you. I could not see you with anyone else so started distancing myself, from you and from my feelings too. But nothing worked." He paused for a while.

"I know you're hurting. But let me tell you, you were not the only one in this situation. My heart was crumbling all this while too. But I was helpless. You were out of my league and I was so very scared. I remember practising how to express my love for you in the mirror for some thousand times, but every time I see you, it flew out of the window." He confessed with tears making his vision blurry.

"I know you can never reciprocate my feelings and I don't want you to either. I never want you to be any awkward around me or to feel sorry for me. They are my feelings and I can deal with them. I know they will disappear slowly." He let out his last sentence very low with a heavy heart and crumbled soul. "Why do you want your feelings to fade away?" She spoke blatantly and he stood there bewildered. She continued, "And why do you even want to run away? What makes you think your existence is worth less than mine? What if I say that right now I just want to run into your arms and never leave you? What if I say that I want you to stay by my side always and protect me like you always did? Do you still want to leave me?"

Without even wasting a second, he pulled her into his arms with the hope of never leaving her. Neither tears stopped, nor did their love. Sometimes confessions are tough but leaving your love seems even tougher. Just take a small step towards your love and it will never let you down.

PRACHI KHANNA

She is a MBA degree holder and a professional banker. Currently completely into writing and have been a freelance content writer for almost 2 years now. After writing for a lot of people she thought of writing for her own self and she found it very interesting to pen down her own thoughts. Although she was a writer since her childhood.

Email ID : pdkscribbles@gmail.com.
Instagram : Pdkscribbles

The Son Of God

During the corona Glitches.
He was amongst mafia Clutches.
Trying to fight against the Hitcher.
Everyone around him proved to be a Ditcher.
They made his home a Buchar.
They are the most powerful and are rich than the Richer.
He was under tremendous Pressure.
He lost his breath and a life as Treasure.
He is watching from Above.
He has got all his fans' Love.
He will get Justice.
No matter how far one has to go for This.
His friends were the moon and the Star.
He is near yet quite Far.
The ones who thought you be Close.
By him only he was given Overdose.
They claim he did this to Himself.
No one hear is dumb and Deaf.
We can see how manipulation has taken Place.
Entire universe is there to Embrace.
They can't run away anymore it's the end of the Race.
It's shame on Human Race.
They lost all their humanity and our looked down by disgrace.
And in turn he won respect and Grace.
Don't forget they all have got almighty to Face.
For them even hell doesn't have a Place.
Till how can they try the facts to Lace.
They all are under the Radar.
Justice is no more Farther.
#SSR

PRANAV M SREEJITH

Hey!, This is Pranav M Sreejith a writer in his early twenties, an engineering student born and bought up in Kannur, Kerala. Writing has been an escape from reality for him and has been doing it since a couple of years, for him the journey began when he was in high school, started from scribbling his anger down on a piece of paper and a couple of years later typing them down on a social platform under the handle @inkeddialect. An year from that day he is now published in over twenty books across the world.

Email ID : inkeddialect@gmail.com

(1)

“I feel like it is almost impossible for us as humans to not judge the things and people around us immediately, it automatically happens inside our brain. BUT it is a choice whether you are open to the possibility of being wrong about the thing or person you judged.”

(2)

“Every time I think I have you nailed down you say something or do something that’s just so unpredictable.” He stroked through hks love’s long hair with one of his quiet smiles. “It just reminds me how much I love you.”

RUTUPURNA SATAPATHY

Rutupurna Satapathy is from Puri, Odisha. She is currently pursuing her graduation final year. She is a passionate writer, a poet, and a content creator. She has been Co Authored many anthologies and has compiled one book. She is a nyctophile and a person who is always high on books.

Email ID : rutuparnasatapathy05@gmail.com.
Instagram Username : rutuparna_satapathy_

Dance

Vagaries of this life
Can be tough and hard to grasp.
And yet have they conquered us fully?
Look how far you have come...
Open your heart to happiness
Let every pure absorb light...
Time goes by and slips away
Just as the sky turns from blue to grey.
Fly in the blueness of sky
Understand that nothing can die...
To live a life...you must want to live..
To want to live...you must find a way...
When all hope is lost..you must stand tall..
When all others retreat ..you must prevail..
Smile for as long as day is..
And laugh just a little bit more..
Because nature is healing..
Breathe slowly, deeply and listen..
Give all your ideas a chance
Let the sun eat down to goodness..
And kick you off and dance..

S.D. RAHEL CHIRU

She is a Selenophile and Uranophile. She loves to hang out .She is someone who is an extrovert .She is an enthusiastic and cheerful person. She loves travelling and also reading books .She loves animals.

Email ID : rahelchiru67@gmail.com
Instagram Username : sekhochiru059

HOSTEL LIFE

You can wake up whenever you feel like queen.
You are treated as a newbie when you enter the hostel.
Later you are seen as nothing.
You get your breakfast at 8 like those criminals.
You get tea and snacks at 12 like those granny.
You get your dinner at 8 like those prisoners.
You get to meet a lot of different people with different perspective.
You get to know and learn simple life hack for simple and easy life .
You can see a lot of people thinking themselves as Ranchoddas Shamladas Chanchad.
You are seen as the last hope like their moms.
You get to see people during the first two week enjoying their life as rich businesspeople.
Later you see that the same person would be lying in the bed for the whole day eating Maggie as a jobless person.
Your weekends are save for cleaning washroom and bathrooms.
You get to know what life is when you stay in hotel.
You tend to know a lot about different cultures and cuisine .
You get to see a different version of life .

SAUMYA MISHRA

Saumya is a humanities student in Isabella Thoburn College in Lucknow. Her interest lies in literature and photography. She's also a volunteer for animal rights and protection.

Email ID : saumyaexellent98@gmail.com
Instagram Username : __s.a.u.m.y.a

(1)

Our contentment is utterly shallow, it's our reasoning with ourselves during failures. It's merely a nutrition to the ego saying, "You weren't incapable", then we find all possible flaws in the goal and the people who achieved it. And worse, the longing to achieve is still there deep down.

(2)

Heartbreak breaks all your emotional breaks.

SAYANI BAG

“Sayani Bag” An amateur writer who wants to explore the writing world. She hails from West Bengal. Currently, she is pursuing B.A. English (Hons) from Calcutta University. She is a co-author of various anthologies like "It's All About Me and You ", " Chand Alfaaz", " My Eternal Love", "Mystical Life", and many more. She loves to dance, paint and explore new places. She writes and paints her soul on @_poetries.of.blue_.

Email ID : bag.sayani2000@gmail.com

Stay

Stay a little longer with me ,
Even we are going to break apart,
Even if your priorities have changed,
Even if you have to leave with someone else,
Let me hold your hands one last time,
Stay a little longer until my fingers are intertwined with yours,
Let me feel the serenity of your lips,
Let me stare at you for a while,
Let us dance to our favorite song,
Let me be yours for one last time,
Stay a little longer even if you are going to break my heart ,
Stay a little longer even if you have reasons to leave,
Stay a little longer, knowing that our story won't last forever,
For the sake of staying with me,
Stay a little longer with me.

Maybe

Our love was a feeling when it started,
It broke me into pieces when you departed,
Maybe those days were tough because you did break my trust
Maybe one day I'll learn to forget you,
Maybe someday I'll stop craving your presence,
Maybe one day I won't long for your phone calls,
Maybe one day I won't get affected on hearing your name,
Maybe one day I'll remove you from my priority list,
Maybe one day I'll stop writing poems about you,
Maybe someday you'll turn the pages of your diary,
You'll find the rose that I gave you,
Maybe it's the situation that has changed,
Maybe the distance between us grew,
Maybe someday you'll realize,
That if you had tried she would have stayed,
You'll realize that you were my happy place,
Maybe someday we'll meet again...
We will meet as different characters in a story,
Maybe in that story, I'll get to call you mine,
Maybe someday our eyes will meet again,
And our hearts won't be strangers then,
May be someday we will meet in our favourite coffee shop,
I'll look in your eyes, and you won't look away,
You will promise me that you'll stay by my side,
Someday we will meet again,
And walk again those paths with hand in hand,
Your hands will fit perfectly into mine,
Your feet will match my long strides,
Maybe in that lifetime, we'll be each other's happily ever after.
And we will be each other's best compatibility.

SHRIYANGANA PYNE

She is a dreamer by mind , a writer by the soul and a kid by heart. She is the kind who is an astrophille , a lover of the stars and astronomy.

Email ID : angina.pyne@gmail.com.
Instagram Username : Shriieazy

Reminiscing And Upgrading

The fear sometimes debilitates and the mind keeps reminiscing.
It dreams about that soul who was an example of perfidy.
It reaches out for helping like a solicitous person still having the tenacity.
The branches of the tree was more bent and the trees became more concrete towards sensitivity.
Laying down the words and keeping the guard done led to ramification.
People around and with considered this a case of demystification.
Hence sailing where the wind took and feeling the chill breeze hitting the face.
All seemed comparatively lighter yet darker.
Minutes seemed to be like months in this grave and prolonged time.
The dark and gigantic clouds pervaded the sky and cast a shadow in the valley.
The Great Banyan Tree seeked to shield the innocent seedling in the downpour dutifully.

Gender Equality

Gender equality is not a travesty
It will prevail as it is our responsibility
It is still pristine but should not be paradoxical.
Time is ripe for everyone to be vocal
Enough of domination and oppression
In the name of salvation
There should be instigating of bringing a revolution
A comprehensive mission to allude a colossal transition
The condescending nature of both men and women imposing
On the opposite gender to proudly flaunt their position is humiliating
That is an upheaval and a sense of intimidation will form in the society
That will get worse and worse so will the frequency
The duration is prolonged but the mindset to overcome it is determination
There should be assertion and not distortion and an action of coercion
Including voicing and educating people about it is the ultimate solution
This entails of not being fearful and carrying out with certitude that requires the skill of persuasion
It facilitates full immersion and intervention
When people view something wrong in the nation
It can be possible if we work as a union
As the world is a haven for expression and perception.

SIDDHI CHANNE

She's that character in the book who is a mixture of fierce and pure and has a really cool weapon of choice: 'the bow and arrow'.

Email ID : combowsid@gmail.com.
Instagram Usernames: @thoughtofit, siddhi_channe

Perspective

Everything in our life is our perspective. Life is defined in different ways by different individuals depending on their experiences. It is said that life is full of problems, struggle, failures and happiness and so we need to prepare ourselves. Also some people believe in "living life " and that it's all about fun. All these people seem to be correct but the where the difference lies is that in one's perspective People think of never-ending struggles are a part of life, some think living life is absolutely doing nothing but enjoying. Everyone just forget that their life has a purpose and all they have to work for is that purpose of our life. Living life is living every single day happily, dealing with our lives in a positive way and doing the job we enjoy wholeheartedly. So all this starts right inside your mind. The way we look at a situation or the way we deal with it is the way we think about it. Our dear mind is really very manipulative. Life is in this moment not in yesterday morning in tomorrow and if we start thinking this way we will be happy all the time, we will tend to make the decisions we should, we will forgive people, we will give our best. It's just the matter of involving your heart, giving your life moments of joy, spreading love and positivity and this is a perspective. Perspective is taking up challenges and not thinking of struggles, it is experiencing everything that comes on your way and not thinking about failures. Happiness can be found in the smallest and simplest of things what matters is just your perspective.

The Game Day

It's the time,
The time to realize and understand the strength within,
To recognize that some loved ones are always with you,
May be not a physical presence but a connection of soul which is beyond boundaries,
To play smart and sharp,
To get the massive confidence out and hit the bull's eye with all might.
Not for today.
But for every single day you worked on,
for that every single day when you decided not to give up and work hard to achieve,
For the days, you want,
'cause you can you will'
You know that..
Believe yourself, have faith
Understand and keep doing it because it is worth it
Live it
Just do it...

SNEHA RAJ

Sneha,from Ranchi Jharkhand. A fifteen year little girl with big dreams! She wants people to know her by words, that she expresses through hard work! Earlier, she didn't took writing as her passion but now she consider it to be her best friend, as it will stay till the end!

Email ID : snehaprasad2204@gmail.com.
Instagram Username : @aeonian_words_

Virginity Test

Elegant bride with delicate bangles,
Self uttering,"Ohh! A perfect bride at all angle!"
And here comes my groom,
Take me to his room.
Where I saw white as the only hue,
He said," These plannings are all for me and you!"
Heart pops out and unconscious feeling within,
Today I am just a different being.
And we turned up that night,
As it was our first wedding night.
And those pure white sheets ,
Were still not red painted!
He asked, "Why this bedsheet is not even painted red,
Should I speak the words I am leaving unsaid?"
And suddenly,
When the face that glowed yesterday night was too bright,
But this morning its filled with fright!
Question arised!
Is it necessary for that bedsheet to change its colour?
Mind explained,
" Virginity test and thats what regarded as purity test",
Not just with you it even goes with rest."
And its all about losing hymen right?
Which is not only lost by having sex.
Losing hymen is not a big deal,
Its lost even by physical activities we take,
So just stop this "Virginity test" for God's sake!

Fixing Things I Never Thought I Have To

Fixing things I never thought I have to fix,
Was living days without even a sparkle of risk.
Thantophobia was never my cup of tea,
As forever I thought was he.
Life went on without any punctuation in it,
All I needed was that happy shit.
Those unwanted feeling don't know of what,
But it still let skip beats of my heart. All around me, happiness I was unable to see.
His absence made me parted from my presence in me.
And, and.....
Today, when I sit... I sit to fix those things,
Those little things,
That I broke by myself and so called broken.
Sorry, I was unable to make this heart shut up the times it said your name.
I would have asked my mind to stop thinking,
And my cheeks to stop blushing over your name.
I would have stopped my hand to reach to my that uncontrollable laughter whenever you said something
hilarious.
I would have asked these eyes not to cry over your sadness and would have also asked it not to talk
through it ways on video calls.
I would have stopped myself from loving you,
Who made me first realize what loving myself was.
And right now,
I should ask my tears to stop falling over this sheet,
And fix those unfulfilled dreams by myself,
Which yours and mine was together as ours.

SNEHAL APTURKAR

Snehal Apturkar is a researcher from Nagpur. She has been a member of American Chemical Society, penned several reports during her post graduate degree program with one of her article published in US International Magazine and another in tapobhoomi magazine. Apart from writing, she has developed a deep interest in dance, sketching, art and public speaking. She's active in social work, she helped several poor families with basic needs.

Email ID : snehalapt96@gmail.com.
Instagram Username : @iam_snehal443 ; @natthesoul

The Phase

"You are an innocent question to which there's no answer," she said smiling in front of the mirror. I'm wondering what she was trying to urge herself into..

She had the person in her life who had a most beautiful life teaching experience, who was fighting with the chances yet living for a purpose, prepared for any and every episode of life. There have been days when she was willing to remain out of the world, lost in her own self which was completely okay to her.

There have been days when she was out socializing all the way but at some point she felt alone and shut everything to be okay. She always watched for these signs, remembered them just like the back of her hands. There have been days when she was fragile that anything would break her, she held herself high saying- it's okay, this too shall pass. There have been days when she felt like crying about something that she remembered from years ago albeit she swore she moved on.

She never tried to elucidate herself to not sleep in the past because that wasn't the time to convince herself, and there have been days when she wanted to be alone. This was a true solid phase in her life that made her realize when to offer herself some space as nothing was in spite of her. The phase that made her stronger than ever, the ruler of her own.

The Woman I Know

People say she's a robust woman, hiding pain behind her smile. She isn't born simple, she has forged through waves of life and overcame every outcome. She has grown into a gorgeous woman with each challenge, mentally and emotionally. She isn't someone who is ashamed of the scars that life has left her with. There is a beauty, wisdom and truth in her scars. Her scars are the proof that she survived the deepest pain when she was down and out.

She told you she'd move on. She told you she'd allow you to go someday. Honestly it had been the toughest thing she had ever done but it had been worthwhile. Her progress was singing to an equivalent song she used to hate a lot, understanding the lyrics deeply. Everything seemed broken then but when life got real it showed her who wasn't! There was a time in her life where situations mattered the foremost not the emotions and she had to beat it although it had been painful. On the other hand she realized it had been the simplest thing to try to.

Maybe, she was counting on a broken mirror, that never allowed her to ascertain her beautiful side, clinging on one rare touch that made her feel safe. You can't choose her pretty sides to stay and therefore the ugly ones to go away. She's a gorgeous story penned compulsively by her own hands. You cannot just open up the story of her life somewhere from the middle, address page 826 to understand her. She fell and she broke but she rose again, to rewrite and keep the book.

SWAGATIKA SAHOO

She is an easy going very ambitious girl from a small town of Titilagarh in Odisha. Currently,she is pursuing MBBS from Ukraine. Her mother has always been her role model in life. If she can inspire atleast one person through her writing it would be an achievement for her.

Email ID : swagatikas124@gmail.com.
Instagram Username : swagatika_124s

Bindi

As a small kid I would always look at my mother getting ready and wearing her red bindi in great awe. After she was gone, I would always try to replicate whatever she did in front of the mirror with the same expressions and with that same red bindi placing it right at the centre of my forehead, just like she did. This ritual continues even today every morning but as I grew up I stopped replicating her because I got busy with school and then I left home for higher studies but whenever I remember her, her beautiful face appears in front of my eyes with that same old red bindi enhancing its charm… I have always found answers to all my problems within my mother. She has been my idol since childhood. I loved the way she handled every little bit flawlessly, from being a strong woman outside home to being an extra affectionate mother inside. My father has always stayed outside home because of his profession, my mother has always taken care of us single handily but I have never seen her struggling, I have always seen her as a graceful lady. I was not able to understand these things when I was small but as I grew up I started noticing fine lines and dark circles on her face, she may be hiding the pain and struggle from us for so long but her age did not let them hidden. Yet, I get emotional and awestricken at the same time to see her carrying that red dot pleasantly at the centre of her eyebrows with an undefinable grace. That bindi defines how flawlessly she has been doing her duty as a wife and a perfect mother. I have never found her bindi smudged, how smoothly she carries so much responsibility on her shoulder just like a super woman. Someday will I be able to be like her? How she does all these? Am I good enough to be like her someday? When I was busy finding the answers of these questions, a vague memory crossed my mind, a memory of my childhood- "one day when I was getting ready in front of the mirror to replicate her, but getting disappointed again and again as I was unable to match her grace. Smilingly she came, removed her bindi and fixed it on my face… at that moment I found the resemblance of my mother's grace in my face." DEDICATED TO U MAA..

Alpenliebe

Have you ever thought about the meaning of alpenliebe? Alpenliebe was the most popular toffee in the 90s with an unique round shape and a mouth-watering caramel flavour.. I still remember those days clear in my mind. No, I am not ranting about my childhood but I am just happy that I have something in my memories which makes me smile everytime I remember those. Alpenliebe was dreamy creamy sweet candy just like my childhood was..and the reason we millenials often seem wanting to go back to those days is because we were the last generation with the least influence of technology in our childhoods. With technology we may have everything right on our finger tips, no one is far away..just a touch and you get connected to someone on the other side of the world..but sadly we are unable to connect with people near us.. This technology has given us power to achieve nearly everything we think of on the other hand it has crippled us, destroyed many childhoods and has left us alone.. I still remember I would wait after having lunch so that my mother would give me a shining 1 rupee coin and I would rush to a small store infront of our house for some candies or toffees.. I could not even pronounce alpenliebe but it was my favourite candy though..usually on birthdays we would wear a new casual dress to school and distribute chocolates ..special ones would get 2 and others will be given only one..that was the greatest joy of all time..and after 3rd standard I was promoted to 2 rupee coin per day..and I usually felt like I could buy anything in that shop..(ps: ambani must be feeling like this while on shopping I think..)I did not knew about a thing like cell phone until I was in 6th standard..and with great awe I would search for its wire like the telephones had..I thought it was magic or something..every evening we would go to each others house and together we would play a lot of games..like today kids,

they too call each other for a match of pubg of course..we may have simplified a lot of things but we don't have time for each other..every face is buried in that phone and no one has the time to look at faces other than on instagram..our moods have become stories and statuses and our parents have turned old school ..we can't even help someone without taking a selfie .. when I was going to meet my school friends after so long..I was getting a flashback of those recess school games everything all way long..but when I reached, every other being was buried in that smartphone, the one which has made us dumb..and after I left from there I saw everyone posting photos with captions like we really miss our childhood and we want to go back. strange but true ...do you really deserve to go back in that time to relive your childhood? You know the answer, we know the answer but we rather chose to go in the flow with this generation instead..and I guess I will let that past me to rest in peace in my memories and enjoy her favourite alpenliebe..

TUSAR RANJAN MAHAPATRA

Very enthusiastic and fun-loving. Engineer by profession, writer and musician by passion, he loves to try out new things just for the sheer fun of it. He loves life and everything and everyone in it.

Email ID : tusar.mahapatra08@gmail.com
Instagram : t_u_5_h_a_r

Savouries of life

Ask the weight of air
To a drowning man
Ask the sweetness of water
To a deserted one
Ask the questions of import
To the deprived people
For even colossal palaces hold
Guilt in excess of a tonne
Such is the lush green around
With worth unknown
For the silent guardians
With gifts reknown
Appreciation amounting
To naught for them
Though worlds they hold
Without condemn
From the chirpy residents
Of the stout foliage
To the magnanimous beasts
Floating in Nature's barge
Being sunk by the multitude
Of our ignorant race
Indifferent of the tears
Drying on the Mother's face
Gone is the beautiful creation
With it, the soulful abode too
For gone are the forests
And with them our future too
Let's commence the amendments
For its never too late
For mistakes to turn into
Saviours of one's fate...

A Poet's Insight

High as the sky though
Rooted strong to the ground
Giving selflessly though
Bestowed with gifts to astound
Irrespective of what the taker is
The giver remains the same
For seeing is not the necessity
If the needy be naught but maim
"What if colours didn't matter?
What if black or white were, but mere names?
What if the world was not so biased?
What if our pains were, but mere games?"
Thinking this through and through
Unbinding the shackles of disgrace
For all the matters in this world is
The blooming heart and not the doomed race...
For all these feelings, words just flow
In a rhythm so unearthly, yet so bright
Every sound one hears
Every touch one makes
All travel through time in
What else but a poet's insight...

UDIT JAIN KOTHARI

Udit Jain, an LLB student from Guwahati is a passionate writer, young enthusiast and he deliberately leaves everyone awestruck by his choice of words. His writings are made with perfect touch of humanity and realism with an impression of optimism. The positivity he creates through his quotes is an impromptu blend of societal obligation. He searches for the right platforms to promote and elevate his writings forte in a direction that he admires and lifts him to the heights of success.

Email ID : udit96jain@gmail.com.
Instagram Username : kingbhai_

Quote 1>

Bring me a lifetime of your laughter and That's all the music I would ever need.

Quote 2>

In life in every step we have to give an exam; and the examiner is the almighty God.

Quote 3>

In the world full of show offs, Be someone's comfort.

Quote 4>

Patience is our ability of how we behave, not just to wait.

Quote 5>

There would be number of hurdles in the journey of life. Let them pass with a smile.

Quote 6>

It's okay to be scared. Being scared means you're about to do something really, really brave.

Quote 7>

Don't create Rivals, create Competitors.

Quote 8>

You are a part of my roots. My art is nothing but an extension of your magic.

Quote 9>

Happiness is not something ready-made. It comes from your own actions.

Quote 10>

There is no peace without suffering; The greater the suffering, the greater the peace.

Quote 11>

You have dug your soul out of the dark,
You have fought to be here;
Do not go back to what buried you.

Quote 12>

In you, I’ve found cities and oceans that I wish to travel. You have stories within you which I wish to live in with you.

Quote 13>

I can imagine no greater heroism than Motherhood.

Quote 14>

It’s not the beards or hairstyles which make him strikingly Charming.
It’s the Courage of him.

Quote 15>

I was asked : What is poison?
- Anything beyond what we need is poison. It can be power, laziness, food, ego, ambition, vanity, fear,anger or whatever.

Quote 16>

Life isn't about finding yourself. Life is about creating yourself.

Quote 17>

Be like a salt
Get mixed easily
But Make your presence feel when you are missing.

Quote 18>

Don't ask me
How much I love you,
If I could measure it,
It wouldn't be true.

Quote 19>

I don't need alcohol to be happy
Her pretty eyes does the trick..!

Quote 20>

Just how the Skies don't regret helping the Earth grow,
And the Sun does not regret helping the Moon glow,
You too should not regret loving our flame,
It is only our love that cannot be tamed.

Quote 21>

Success is not owned, it is rented,
And that rent is due everyday.

Quote 22>

The World has enough Jokers, be a King.

Quote 23>

I wanna be old with you,
Not with your memories in my heart.

Quote 24>

In a world full of copies
Be an original.

Quote 25>

A healthy relationship cures people,
An unhealthy relationship hurts people.
Do yourself a favour and stay out of harm's way.

Conclusion

We would like to thank all the readers who have devoted their precious time in reading this book. It's a great pleasure for us if you found the book useful. It's a great feeling to write on the Open Theme in an Amazing Book named CREATIVE SPARKS which can bring a change in you or in your life only by reading this book. All the write-ups are the combination of contents from different co-authors who have written their amazing creativity.

Flairs and Glairs, a platform by a student for the students. We are esteemed youth struggling to carve out our path for our future and we follow a basic mindset Since everyone is not born with all-round skills. Joining hands with people who are born to execute it with perfection is the best way to evolve. Self-Evolution is the need of the hour but, evolving as a community is what we strive for. The initiative as kickstarted by, Founder- Mr. Shubham Shah with the motive to utilize the skillset and talent of writing has now a team of 10+ people who are actively participating into newer forms of learning and discovering talents among youngsters. We Provide platform and services like Publishing opportunities, Open mics, Workshops, Hands-on training. Operating with Brand Name of Flairs and Glairs (Publication House), we offer the chance of elevating a passionate writer to an esteemed author With Brand name Teekhe Zasbaaat. We bring to you an opportunity to get accustomed with the Public Speaking and Presenting of Thoughts along with regular challenges to brush up your inking spirit. The newest initiative to extend our services we introduced in a new writing Platform- The Glittering Fables and Ink Over Tears.

We Choose to Fly Like A Falcon than to be

a Leg Pulling Crab.

To Know More: Infoline – 7781900870
Mail Us At-
flairsandglairs@gmail.com / info@flairsandglairs.in
Or Visit is at
www.flairsandglairs.com / www.flairsandglairs.in
Social Handles- @flairsandglairs @teekhezasbaaat

www.ingramcontent.com/pod-product-compliance
Ingram Content Group UK Ltd.
Pitfield, Milton Keynes, MK11 3LW, UK
UKHW022004190726
13853UKWH00004B/1718

9 789390 799145